LUCIUS SHEPARD

THE
TABORIN
SCALE

A NOVELLA OF THE
DRAGON GRIAULE

THE
TABORIN
SCALE

A NOVELLA OF THE
DRAGON GRIAULE

Lucius Shepard

SUBTERRANEAN PRESS 2010

First Edition

ISBN
978-1-59606-288-7

Subterranean Press
PO Box 190106
Burton, MI 48519

www.subterraneanpress.com

CHAPTER

ONE

I F A MAN CAN be measured by the size of his obses sions, George Taborin might have been said to be a very small man, smaller even than the quartermen rumored to inhabit the forests of Tasmania. He was a numismatist by trade, by avocation a lover of rare and ancient coins, and he spent his days cataloguing, cleaning, and in contemplation of such coins, picturing as he did the societies whose lifeblood they had emblematized. Rubbing the face of Ptolemy, for instance, on a silver drachma found in Alexandria, struck at the approximate time of the invasion of Cyprus by Demetrios Poliokortes (probably in Salamis, the last city to fall to the Besieger), would conjure not merely the historical context of the Roman empire and Ptolemaic Egypt, but brought visions so vivid that he imagined he felt the weight of an armored breastplate on his chest or caught the scent of naphtha from an arrow dipped in Greek fire smoldering in its victim's flesh. It was as if the ball of his thumb stirred the energies of the coin, releasing some essence of the moments through which it had passed, and it had been thus ever since his sixth birthday when his uncle gave him a Phoenician copper as a present.

From this you might suppose George, in his fortieth year, to have been a fastidious, obsessive little man given to wool-gathering, with spectacles and a potbelly and few close friends, his minimal life partitioned into orderly sections like the trays whereon he displayed the best of his collection. You would have been correct in this assessment save for one thing: George Taborin was not little. He stood a hand's breadth over six feet, more if you measured from the peak of his coarse black hair, which tended to arrange itself into spiky growths when left unwashed, causing it to be said that if George ran into you while walking with his head down (as was his habit), you would be fortunate to survive the encounter without a puncture or two. Thanks to his parents, a farm couple who had viewed him less as a beloved addition to the family than as child labor, he was powerfully built; his sedentary occupation had eroded his strengths and softened his mid-section, but not so much that he was often challenged—he had earned a schoolyard reputation for toughness and durability in a fight and that reputation clung to him yet. He had a slightly undershot chin, a straight nose whose only notable quality was that it was too big for his face, and a mouth through which he was prone to breathe due to a persistent sinus condition (for all that, his was a face that missed being handsome by an ounce here, a centimeter there, and might have passed muster had there been more self-confidence underlying it). These features conspired with his bulk to lend him a doltish aspect, like a gangling idiot boy thickened into a man. When gazing into a mirror, something he did as infrequently as possible, he would have the notion that his soul had not thickened commensurately and was rattling around inside its house, a poor fit for the flesh it animated, stunted and too small by half.

Pursuant to his family's wishes (the thought being that if George didn't marry young he would never find a woman), at the age of fifteen he wed Rosemary LeMaster, a chubby, sullen, unprepossessing girl who, over the course of a quarter-century, had matured into a flirtatious, Rafael-esque matron. They had not been blessed with children and, because George deeply desired a family, as did Rosemary (so she claimed, though he suspected her of taking steps to ensure her infertility), they still shared the marriage bed once a week, regular as clockwork; but now that George's business (Taborin Coins & Antiquities) had prospered, providing them the wherewithal to hire servants, Rosemary, freed from domestic duties, wasted no time in making up for the period of youthful experimentation she'd never had, aligning herself with a clutch of upper middle-class wives in Port Chantay who called their group the Whitestone Rangers (named for the district in which many of them lived) and considered themselves prettier, more sophisticated and fashionable than they in fact were. She veered into a social orbit of parties and trivial causes (the placing of planter boxes along the harbor, for one) that served as opportunities to meet the men with whom she and her sisters would share dalliances and affairs. Although troubled by his wife's infidelities (he had no proof positive, yet he was aware of the Rangers' liberal attitude toward the matrimonial bond), George did not complain. He and Rosemary led essentially separate lives and this latest separation had not created any disruption in the routines of the marriage. Then, too, he had no grounds for complaint since he was regularly unfaithful to Rosemary.

In the spring of each year, George would travel to Teocinte and pass the next three weeks sporting in the brothels of Morningshade, a district that never received the morning sun, tucked so close beneath the dragon Griaule's[1] monstrous shadow, his ribcage bulged out over a portion of the area like a green-and-gold sky.[2]

---

1   The mile-long dragon, paralyzed by a wizard's spell, in whose lee Teocinte had grown.

2   Portions of this sky, scales shed by the dragon, would occasionally fall on the rooftops below, crushing the houses beneath,

Apart from its brothels, Morningshade was known for its junk shops and stalls where you could find antiquities and relics of Griaule (mostly fakes) among the dragon-shaped pipes and pendants, his image adorning a variety of merchandise including plates, pennants, toys (wooden swords were a big seller), tablecloths, teaspoons, mugs and maps purporting to divulge the location of his horde.[3] George would spend his afternoons combing through these shops, searching for old coins. One evening in May, after such an expedition, he took himself to Ali's Eternal Reward (the crudely-lettered word "Hellish" had been added and marked for insertion between Ali's and Eternal), a brothel on the sunnier edge of Morningshade, there to examine his day's treasures over a pint of bitters.

The common room of the tavern, lit by kerosene lamps and almost empty at that early hour, was shaped like a capital I and smelled of fried onions, stale beer and

---

causing the plots of land upon which they had stood to appreciate in value because they would be unlikely to experience another such disaster.

3   As the tale was told, over the centuries people came from the ends of the earth to lay offerings before him, and these offering had been transported by a succession of creatures and men controlled by the dragon to a hiding place known only to him (its location having been subsequently erased from the minds of his minions). The treasure was said by some to be fabulous beyond belied, and by others to be a complete fabrication.

several decades of grease. Pitch-covered beams quartered the ceiling, beneath which lay benches and boards, and whitewashed walls gone a splotchy gray from kitchen smoke and innumerable grimy touches, and a counter behind which a corpulent barman wearing a fez (not Ali, who was a purely fictive personage) stood lordly and watchful, punctuating the quiet with the occasional *thwack* of a flyswatter. Three young women in loosely belted dressing gowns sat at the center of the room, talking softly. Carts rattled by outside, and a vendor shrilled the virtues of her coconut sweets. To George, sitting at a window in a rear corner of the I, the conversations of passers-by came as bursts of unintelligible words peppered with curses.

While inspecting the contents of a glass jar containing coins and buttons and tin badges that he had purchased as a lot, he unearthed a dark leathern chip stiff with age and grime, shaped like a thumbnail, though three times the size and much thicker. He opened his cleaning kit and dabbed at the chip with a cotton ball dipped in solvent, after some exercise clearing a speck of bluish green at the center. His interest enlisted, he put on the spectacles he used for close work, bent to the chip and rubbed at it vigorously with the cotton ball, widening the speck. The blue-green color held a gem-like luster. He fitted a jeweler's loupe to his spectacles and held the chip to his eye.

"What you got there?"

A prostitute clad in a robe of peach silk, a thin brunette in her early twenties with curly hair, a dusky complexion and a face that, though pretty, was too sharp-featured for his tastes, slid onto the bench beside him and held out a hand. "Can I see?"

Startled not only by her, but by the fact that the tavern had, without his notice, filled with a noisy crowd, he dropped the chip into her hand, an action he instantly regretted, worried that she might abscond with it.

"I haven't seen one of these since I was a bare-ass kid," the woman said, pushing her hair back from her eyes. "My granny wore one like this around her neck. She promised she'd leave it to me, but they buried the old hag with it."

"You know what it is, then?"

"A dragon scale...not off a monster like Griaule. The babies have this blue color when they're born, or so I hear[4]. I suppose it could be Griaule's from when he was little. There ain't been any baby dragons around these parts for centuries. The scale my granny wore was passed down from her great-great-great."

George reached for the scale, but the woman closed her hand.

---

4   This was true only as so far as dragons native to the region went. Dragons bred in other climes displayed a variety of coloration, ranging from ivory-scaled snow dragons of the Antarctic to the reddish-gold hue of those dragons that once inhabited the wastes north of Lake Baikul, a shade that deepened to a rich bronze at maturity.

THE TABORIN SCALE

"I'll give you a ride for it." She opened her robe, exposing her breasts, and shimmied her shoulders.

"Let me have it," said George, snapping his fingers.

"Don't act so stern!" She jiggled the scale in her palm, as if assessing its weight, and then passed it to him. "Tell you what. I'll give you liberties for a week. When you go back to Port Chantay, you'll have more than a guided tour of Griaule to remember, I promise."

"How can you tell I'm from Port Chantay?"

With a disdainful sniff, she said, "I have a gift."

Her breasts were fuller than he had thought, quite shapely, with large cinnamon areolae. Ever a pragmatic sort when it came to business affairs, he reckoned the scale to be a curiosity piece, not worth that much to the run of his customers; but he pressed his seller's advantage.

"I'm here two more weeks," he said. "Put yourself at my disposal for that time and the scale is yours."

"At your disposal? You'll have to speak plainer than that. I ain't letting you tie me up, if that's how you're bent."

"I'm staying at the Weathers. I'd want you there with me."

"The Weathers," she said, and made an appreciative face. "What else would you want?"

George spelled out his needs in clinical detail; the woman nodded and said, "Done."

She extended a hand and, as if imitating George, snapped her fingers. "Give it here."

"When the two weeks are up. One of us will have to trust the other to fulfill their end of the bargain. I'd prefer it be you."

CHAPTER TWO

WITH THE DEATH OF the dragon Griaule, the city council of Teocinte were forced to confront a question they had failed to anticipate: When dealing with a creature whose heart beat once every thousand years, how does one determine whether he is actually dead? Since the sole perceptible sign of death was the closing of his eyes, it was suggested that he had merely lapsed into a coma induced by the countless gallons of poisoned paint slapped onto his side during the creation of Meric Cattanay's mural[5]. The parasites that lived

---

[5]   The process by which Griaule purportedly had been killed took more than 30 years to complete and was achieved by the utilization of arsenic- and lead-based paints in a mural painted on his side. The manufacture of these paints had destroyed the lush forests of the Carbonales (a steady supply of timber was necessary

on and inside him had not fled the body and there was no evidence of corruption (nor would there be for many years if the rate of decay were as glacially slow as the rest of his metabolic processes). Indeed, it had been ventured that since Griaule was a magical being, the possibility existed that his corpse would prove to be uncorrupting.

Decades before, when the council accepted Cattanay's plan, they had acted in confidence and contracted with various entrepreneurs for the disposal of Griaule's corpse, selling it piecemeal in advance of his death, thus adding millions to the town coffers; but the current council regretted their predecessors' decision and refused to honor the contracts[6]. Due to their uncertainty about his

---

to heat the vats in which the paint was distilled) and placed such a stress on the economy that a number of wars had been fought with neighboring city-states in order to replenish Teocinte's exchequer.

6   Cele Van Alstyne of Port Chantay, who had secured the rights to Griaule's heart, estimated to weigh nine million pounds, was desperate to revive her failing pharmaceutical company and initiated legal action. She was joined in this by a group of speculators who had bought the approximately one hundred and sixty million pounds of bones (except for the skull, sold to the King of neighboring Temalagua) and planned to export them to foreign countries for use as sexual remedies, charms, souvenirs, etc.; and by a second consortium who had bought the skin, all two hundred and twenty million pounds of it (not counting the mural, destined to be housed in the Cattanay Museum). Lawyers for the council fought a delaying action, claiming that since the dragon's death could not be proven absolutely, the lawsuits were invalid.

mortal condition, they still feared Griaule. If he were alive, they could only imagine his reaction to an attempted dissection. Then there was the matter of aesthetics. Thanks to the discovery of mineral springs south of town and, in no small part, to Griaule himself, Teocinte had become a tourist destination. Turning a portion of the town into an abattoir, with several hundred thousand tons of dragon meat and guts and bones lying about, would be an inappropriate advertisement for fun and relaxation. The council was hesitant to act, yet the citizenry of Teocinte, who for generations had lived under Griaule's ineffable dominion, clamored for an official judgment. It was a touchy situation, one that demanded a delicate resolution, and therefore the council tried—as do all accomplished politicians—to make doing next to nothing seem like a compromise. They tore down the scaffolding Cattanay had erected in order to create his mural, scoured the moss from the teeth, cut away the vegetation from his body, leaving in place only the thickets surrounding the ruin of Hangtown on his back (now uninhabited except for a caretaker), which they designated a historical site. They constructed rope walkways leading to every quarter of the dragon and offered tours, inducing tourists to go where most of the townspeople feared to tread. This, they thought, would promote the idea that they believed Griaule to be dead, yet would provide no evidentiary proof and put off a final determination. If Griaule were still alive and a few tourists died as a result of this experiment in the social dynamic, well, so be it. They further built several luxury hotels, among them the Seven Weathers, on the slopes of Haver's Roost, each offering excellent views of the dragon. And so, on the day after he found the scale, George stood at a window in his suite at the Weathers, sipping coffee and having a morning cigar, gazing at Griaule: an enormous green-and-gold lizard looming like a hill with an evil head over the smoking slum in his shadow, his tail winding off between lesser hills, light glinting from the tip of a fang and coursing along the ribbing of the sagittal crest rising from his neck, the mural on its side glazed with sun, making it indecipherable at that angle. The huge paint vats that had occupied the flat portion of his skull had been dismantled so as not to distract from the dramatic view.

The woman, Sylvia[7], stirred in the bedroom and George sat down at a writing desk and took up cleaning the scale once again, thinking he might as well make it nice for her. The dirt on the scale was peculiarly resistant and he had managed to clear only a small central patch, about a quarter of its surface, when Sylvia entered, toweling her hair, wearing only sandals and a pair of

---

7   She had adopted this *nom d'amour* after George expressed dissatisfaction with the first name she gave, Ursula, and a selection process that winnowed the choices down to three: Otile, Amaryllis, and Sylvia. He had settled on the latter because it reminded him of a grocer's wife he had admired in Port Chantay, a woman from the extreme south of the country, a region "Sylvia" also claimed as home.

beige lounging trousers. She dropped heavily into the armchair beside the desk and sighed. He acknowledged her with a nod and bent to his task. She made an impatient noise, which he ignored; she flung her legs over the arm of the chair, the towel slipping down onto her thighs, and said blithely, "Well, you don't fuck like a shopkeeper, I'll say that much for you."

Amused, he said, "I assume that's intended as an endearment."

"A what-ment?"

"Praise of a kind."

She shrugged. "If that's how you want to take it."

"So..." He scraped at a fleck of stubborn grime with a fingernail. "How do shopkeepers fuck?"

"With most of them, it's like they're embarrassed to be between my legs. They want to get it over quick and be gone. They turn their backs when they button their trousers. And they don't want me saying nothing while they're riding." She shook out her wet hair. "Not that they don't want me making noises. They like that well enough."

"Then that raises the question: How do I fuck?"

"Like a desperate man."

"Desperate?" He kept on rubbing at the scale. "Surely not."

"Maybe desperate's not the right word." She lazily scratched her hip. "It's like you truly needed what I had to offer, and not just my tra-la-la. I could tell you wanted me to be myself and not some Sylvia."

"I expect I did." He was making good progress—the blue portion of the scale had come to resemble an aerial view of a river bordered by banks of mud and black earth. "From now on I'll call you Ursula."

"That's not my proper name, either."

"What is it, then?"

"You don't want to hear—it's horrible." She stretched like a cat on its back in the sun; her face, turned to the window, blurred with brightness. "Truth be told, I don't mind being Sylvia. Suits me, don't you think?"

"Mmm-hmm."

She lapsed into silence, watching him work, attentive to the occasional squeak his cloth made on the scale, and then she said, "Do you fancy me? I mean, the way I'm talking with you now?"

He cocked an eye toward her.

"I'm curious is all," she said.

"I have to admit you're growing on me."

"I was thinking I might try being myself more often. Always having to be someone else is an awful pressure." She scrambled to her knees in the chair, the towel falling away completely, and leaned over the desk, peering at the scale. "Oh, that blue's lovely! How long you reckon 'til it's done?"

"I'll give it a polish once it's clean. A week or so."

She bent closer, her breasts grazing the desktop, holding her hair back from her eyes, fixed on the streak of blue dividing the scale. How different she seemed from the brittle businesswoman he had met at Ali's! She had tried to sustain that pose, but she let it drop more and more frequently, revealing the country girl beneath. He suspected he knew the basics of her story—a farm family with too many children; sold to a brothel keeper; earning her way by the time she was twelve—and thought knowing the specifics might uncover a deeper compatibility. But that, he reminded himself, was what she would want him to think in hopes of getting a bigger tip. Such was the beauty of whores: No matter how devious, how subtle their pretense, you always knew where you stood with them. He studied her face, prettied by concentration, and absently stroked the scale with his thumb.

A sound came to him, barely audible, part hiss, part ripping noise, as of some fundamental tissue, something huge and far away, cleaved by a cosmic sword (or else it was something near at hand, a rotten piece of cloth parting from the simple strain of being worn, giving way under a sudden stress). This sound was accompanied by a vision unlike any he had heretofore known: It was if the objects that composed the room, the heavy mahogany furniture, the cream-colored wallpaper with its pattern of sailing vessels, the entire surround, were in fact a sea of color and form, and this sea was now rapidly withdrawing, rolling back, much as the ocean withdraws from shore prior to a tidal wave. As it receded, it revealed neither the floors and walls of adjoining rooms nor the white buildings of Teocinte, but a sun-drenched plain with tall lion-colored grasses and stands of palmetto, bordered on all sides by hills forested with pines. They were marooned in the midst of that landscape, smelling its vegetable scents, hearing the chirr and buzz of insects, touched by the soft intricacy of its breezes...and then it was gone, trees and plain and hills so quickly erased, they might have been a painted cloth whisked away, and the room was restored to view. George was left gaping at a portmanteau against the far wall. Sylvia, arms crossed so as to shield her breasts, squatted in the easy chair, her eyes shifting from one point to another.

"What did you do?" she asked in a shaky voice. She repeated the question accusingly, shrilly, as if growing certain of his complicity in the event.

"I didn't do anything." George looked down at the scale.

"You rubbed it! I saw you!" She wrested the scale from him and rubbed it furiously; when nothing came of her efforts she handed it back and said, "You try."

It had not escaped George that there might be a correspondence between the apparition of the plain and the visions that arose when he rubbed his thumb across the face of a coin; but none of those visions had supplied the sensory detail of this last and no one else had ever seen them. He experienced some trepidation at the thought of trying it again and dropped the scale into his shirt pocket.

"Finish dressing," he said. "Let's go down to breakfast."

A flash of anger ruled her face. He folded his pen-knife and packed up his cleaning kit and pocketed them as well.

"Won't you give it one more rub?" she asked.

He ignored her.

Wrapping the towel around her upper body, she gave him a scornful look and flounced into the bedroom.

George sipped his coffee and discovered it was tepid. Through the thin fabric of his shirt, the scale felt unnaturally cold against his chest and he set it on the desk. It might be more valuable than he had presumed. He nudged it with the tip of a finger—the room remained stable.

Sylvia re-entered, still wearing the towel and still angry, though she tried to mask her anger behind a cajoling air. "Please! Give it one little rub." She kissed the nape of his neck. "For me?"

"It frightened you the first time. Why are you so eager to repeat the experience?"

"I wasn't frightened! I was startled. You're the one who was frightened! You should have seen your face."

"That begs the question: Why so eager?"

"When Griaule makes himself known, you'd do well to pay heed or misfortune will follow."

He leaned back, amused. "So you believe this nonsense about Griaule being a god."

"It ain't nonsense. You'd know it for true if you lived here." Hands on hips, she proceeded to deliver what was obviously a quoted passage: "He was once mortal, long-lived yet born to die, but Griaule has increased not only in size, but in scope. Demiurge may be too great a word to describe an overgrown lizard, yet surely he is akin to such a being. His flesh has become one with the earth. He knows its every tremor and convulsion. His thoughts roam the plenum, his mind is a cloud that encompasses our world. His blood is the marrow of time. Centuries flow through him, leaving behind a residue that he incorporates into his being. Is it any wonder he controls our lives and knows our fates?"[8]

"That sounds grand, but it proves nothing. What's it from?"

"A book someone left at Ali's."

"You don't recall its name?"

"Not so I could say."

"And yet you memorized the passage."

"Sometimes there's not much to do except sit around. I get bored and I read. Sometimes I write things."

"What kind of things?"

---

8   The excerpt is from the preface to Richard Rossacher's *Griaule Incarnate*. Rossacher, a young medical doctor, while studying Griaule's blood derived from it a potent narcotic that succeeded in addicting a goodly portion of the population of the Temalaguan littoral. After experiencing an epiphany of sorts, he became evangelic as regarded the dragon and spent his last years writing and proselytising about Griaule's divinity.

"Little stories about the other girls, like. All sorts of things." She caressed his cheek "Try again! Please!"

With a show of patience tried that was only partly a show, expecting that nothing (or next to nothing) would occur; he picked up the scale and ran his thumb along the lustrous blue streak, pressing down hard. This time the ripping sound was louder and the transition from hotel room to sun-drenched plain instantaneous. He fell thuddingly among the tall grasses, the chair beneath him having vanished, and lay grasping the scale, squinting up at the diamond glare of the sun and a sky empty of clouds, like a sheet of blue enamel. Sylvia made a frightened noise and clutched his shoulder as he scrambled to his knees. She said something that—his mind dominated by an evolving sense of dismay—he failed to register. The smells that had earlier seemed generic, a vague effluvia of grass and dirt, now were particularized and pungent, and the sun's heat was no longer a gentle warmth, but an ox-roasting presence. A droplet of sweat trickled down his side from his armpit. Insects whirred past their heads and a hawk circled high above. This was no vision, he told himself. The scale had transported them somewhere, perhaps to another section of the valley. In the distance stood a ring of rolling, forested hills enclosing the lumpish shapes of lesser, nearby hills—his coach had traversed similar hills as it ascended from the coastal plain toward Teocinte, though those had been denuded of vegetation. Panic inspired him to rub at the scale, hoping to be transported back to the room; but his actions proved fruitless.

Sylvia sank to the ground and lowered her head, and this display of helplessness served to stiffen George's spine, engaging his protective instincts. He scanned the valley for signs of life.

"We should find shelter," he said dazedly. "And water."

She made an indefinite noise and half-turned her head away.

"Perhaps there's water there." He pointed to the far-off hills. "And a village."

"I doubt we'll find a village."

"Why not?"

"Don't you recognize where we are?" She waved dejectedly at the closest hill, which lay behind them on the right. "There's Haver's Roost, where the Weathers stood. And the rise over yonder is where Griaule's head rested. The sunken area to the left, with all the shrimp plants and cabbage palms—that's where Morningshade used to lie. There's Yulin Grove. It's all there except the houses and the people."

She continued her cataloging of notable landmarks and he was forced to admit that she was correct. He would have expected her to be upset by this development, fearful and verging on hysteria; but she was outwardly calm (calmer than he), albeit dejected. He asked why she was so unruffled.

"We're accustomed to such doings around here," she replied. "It's Griaule's work. The scale...he must have shed it when he was young and it wound up in that jar. For some reason he set you to find it. So you could clean it and rub on it, I imagine."

In reflex he said, "That's ridiculous."

With a loose-armed gesture toward Haver's Roost, she said, "Teocinte is gone. How else do you think it happened?"

Aside from grass swaying, palmetto fronds lifting in the wind, birds scattering about the sky, the land was empty. Odd, he thought, that birds would act so carefree with a hawk in the vicinity. Shielding his eyes against the glare, he tried to spot the hawk, but it had vanished against the sun field. His uneasiness increased.

"We can't stay here," he said.

Sylvia arranged her towel into a makeshift blouse and appeared to be awaiting instruction.

A bug zinged past George's ear—he swatted at it half-heartedly. "Which way should we go?"

She tugged at a loose curl, a gesture that conveyed a listless air—it had become apparent that she had surrendered herself to Griaule or to some other implausible agency. George grabbed her by the wrist and pulled her to him.

"If this is where Teocinte stood, you know where we can find water," he said

Sullenly she said, "There should be a creek over that way somewhere." She pointed toward the depression in which Morningshade had once sprawled. "It was filthy last I saw it, but now, with nobody around, the water ought to be all right."

"Let's go," he said, and when she showed no sign of complying, he shoved her forward. She swung her fist, striking him in the forehead, an impact that caused her to cry out in pain and cradle her hand.

"Are you angry?" he asked. "Good."

"Don't go pushing me!" she said tearfully. "I won't have it!"

"If you're going to act like your spine's been sucked out, I'll push you whenever I choose," he said. "You can mope about and wait to die on your own time."

CHAPTER
THREE

B Y THE TIME THEY had hiked a third of the distance to the creek, George's practical side had re-established dominance and he had developed a scheme for survival in case their situation, whatever it might be[9], failed to reverse itself. But as he prepared for a solitary life with Sylvia (of whatever duration), planning a shelter that could be added to over the months and years, and devising ways in which they

---

9   Though a rift in time or dimensionality would seem to be indicated, George subscribed to the theory espoused by Peri Haukkola, holder of the Carbajal Chair of Philosophy at the University of Helvetia. Haukkola believed that people under extreme stress could alter the physical universe even to the point of creating pocket realities, and George assumed that a reality formed by Sylvia's self-avowed identity crisis comprised the relatively empty landscape they currently inhabited.

could usefully occupy their time, the hawk reappeared above, swelling to such a size as it dropped toward them that George could no longer believe it was a hawk or any familiar predator. He scooped up Sylvia by the waist, lifting her off the ground, and began to run, ignoring her shrieks, just as a dragon swooped low overhead, coming so near that they felt the wind of its passage. Its scales glinting bright green and gold, the dragon banked in a high turn and arrowed toward them again, and then, with a furious beating of its jointed wings, landed facing them in the tall grasses no more than fifty feet away. It dipped its snout and roared, a complicated noise like half-a-dozen lions roaring not quite in unison. George glimpsed a drop of orange brilliance hanging like a jewel in the darkness of its gullet and threw Sylvia to the ground, covering her with his body, expecting flames to wash over them. When no flames manifested, he lifted his head. The dragon maintained its distance, breath chuffing like an overstrained engine—it seemed to be waiting for them to act. Sylvia complained and George eased from atop her. When she saw the dragon she moaned and put her face down in the grass.

Taking care to avoid sudden movements, George climbed to his feet. He was so afraid, so weak in the knees, he thought he might have to sit down, but he maintained a shaky half-crouch. The dragon's lowered head was almost on a level with his, but its back and crest rose much higher. He estimated it to be twenty-five feet long, perhaps a touch more, from the tip of the tail to its snout. The green-and-gold scales fit cunningly to its musculature, a tight overlay like the scales of a pangolin. It emitted a rumbling, its mouth opening to display fangs longer than his arms. A dry, gamey scent seemed to coil about him like a tendril, causing a fresh tightness in his throat. Yet for all its wicked design and innate enmity, there was something of the canine in the way it cocked its head and scrutinized them, like a puppy (one the size of a cottage) confounded by a curious pair of bugs.

"Sylvia." He reached down, groping for her, his fingers brushing her towel.

In response he received a weak, "No."

"If it wanted to kill us, it would have done so by now," he said without the least confidence.

Not taking his eyes from the dragon, he groped again, caught her wrist and yanked her up. She buried her face in his shoulder, refusing to look at the dragon. Putting an arm about her waist, he steered her back in the direction from which they had come, experiencing a new increment of dread with each step. They had gone no more than thirty feet when, with a percussive rattling of its wings, the dragon scuttled ahead of them, cutting them off. It settled on its haunches and gave forth with a grumbling noise and tossed its head to the side. Sylvia squeaked and George was too frightened to think. Again the dragon tossed its head and loosed a full-throated roar that bent the nearby grasses. Sylvia and

George clung together, their eyes closed. The dragon lifted its snout to the sky and screamed—the trebly pitch and intensity of the cry seemed to express frustration. It tossed its head a third and a fourth time, all to the same side, gestures that struck George as exaggerated and deliberate. Taking a cue from them, he went a couple of halting steps in the direction they indicated, dragging Sylvia along. The dragon displayed neither approval nor disapproval, so George continued on this path, heading toward the rise where Griaule's massive head once had rested.

So began a faltering march, the two of them stumbling over broken ground, harried along by the dragon's rumbles, herded from the former site of Teocinte, past the rise and out onto a vast plain of yellowish green thickets and sugarloaf hills, crisscrossed by animal tracks. On occasion the dragon bulled ahead of them to divert their course, flattening wide swaths of vegetation. The heat grew almost unbearable and George's grip on reality frayed to the point that once, when they stopped to rest and the dragon urged them on with a roar, he sprang to his feet and shouted at the beast. After what must have been several hours of sweat and torment, they reached a spot where a stream widened into a clear pool some eighty or ninety feet across at the widest, flowing into other, smaller ponds and fringed by towering sabal palms, hedged by lesser trees and bushes, a cool green complexity amid the desert of thorny bushes and prickly weeds. There the dragon abandoned them, belching out a final cautionary (thus George characterized it) roar and soaring up into the sky until it once again appeared no bigger than a hawk and vanished into a cloud, leaving them exhausted and stunned, relieved yet despairing. They bathed in the largest pool and felt somewhat refreshed. As night fell, George picked shriveled oranges from a tree beside the pool and they made a meal of nuts and fruit. Shortly thereafter, too fatigued to talk, they fell asleep.

In the morning they had a discussion about returning to the spot to which they had been transported, but the sight of the dragon circling overhead ended that conversation and George began constructing a lean-to from bamboo and vines and palmetto fronds, while Sylvia set herself to catch fish, a task for which she claimed an aptitude. After watching her for half an hour, bent over and motionless in the pool, waiting for the fish to forget her presence and attempting to scoop them up when they swam between her legs, he held out little hope for a fish dinner; but to his amazement, when next he checked in on her he saw that she had caught two medium-sized perch.

That night, with enough of a breeze to keep off the mosquitoes, the two of them reclining on a bed of fronds and banana leaves inside the shelter, gazing at the lacquered reflection of a purple sky so thickly adorned with stars, it might have been a theatrical backdrop, a silk cloth embroidered with sequins...that night their predicament was reduced to a shadow in George's mind by these comforts and a full belly; but it became apparent that Sylvia did not feel so at ease with things, for when he tried to draw her into an embrace, she resisted him vigorously and said, "We're at death's door and that's all you can think about?"

"We're not at death's door," said George. "The dragon was rather solicitous of our welfare. He could have conveyed us to a far more inhospitable spot."

"Be that as it may, we're not exactly sitting pretty."

"Oh, I don't know. One of us is." George gave a broad wink, attempting to jolly her with this compliment.

Sylvia returned a withering look.

"We might as well make the best of things," said George.

She sniffed. "To my mind, making the best of it would include figuring a way out of this mess."

"We had a bargain," George said weakly.

"Back in Teocinte we had a bargain. Here all bets are off."

"I don't see it that way."

"Well, I do...and I'm in charge of the sweet shop. I don't have my medicines with me and I won't risk getting pregnant out here. When we return to Teocinte, I'll do right by you. Until then you'll have to take care of your own needs. And I'll thank you to not do so in my presence."

A pour of wind rustled the thatched roof of the shelter, carrying a spicy scent. Despite understanding that Sylvia's reaction was to be expected, George's feelings were hurt.

"This is your fault," he said glumly.

She sat up, her face pale and simplified by the starlight. "What?"

He sketched out Peri Haukkola's theory concerning the effects of stress on consensus reality.

"You say I'm ridiculous to blame this on Griaule," she said. "Then you put forward this Haukkerman as if..."

"Haukkola."

"...as if it were proof of something. As if because he wrote some stupid theory down, it must be true. And I'm the ridiculous one?" She gave a sarcastic laugh. "You saw the dragon, I assume?"

"Of course! That's just more evidence in support of Haukkola. You're obsessed with Griaule, so you incorporated one of his little friends into your fantasy."

Dumfounded, Sylvia stared at him. "The dragon *is* Griaule! Didn't you notice he's got the same coloring, the same head shape? True, he's not all nicked up and scarred, and he's quite a bit smaller. But it's him, all right."

"You can distinguish between lizards?" He chuckled.

"I've been looking at Griaule most of my life and I can distinguish him." She turned onto her side, showing him her back. "You and Haukkola! You're both idiots! If it helps you to blame me, fine. I'm going to sleep."

CHAPTER
FOUR

THE WIND DIED SHORTLY before dawn and mosquitoes swarmed the interior of the shelter, waking Sylvia and George, driving them into the water for cover. The sun climbed higher and they sat beside the pool, miserable, baking in the heat. Having nothing better to do, George shored up the walls of the shelter and elevated the ceiling, making it less of a lean-too, and then went off foraging. To avoid the thickets, the thorn bushes and the gnats, he followed the meanders of the stream through stands of bamboo and clusters of palmettos with parched brownish fronds. Once he sighted the dragon circling above the plain and lay flat until it passed from view. From that point on, for the better part of an hour, his thoughts became a grim drone accompanying his exertions. At length he happened upon a patch of dirt and grass enclosed by dense brush, an oval of relative coolness and shade cast by a solitary mango tree with ripening fruit hanging from its boughs in chandelier-like clusters. He fashioned his shirt into a sling and had begun loading it with mangos when he saw two figures slipping through the brush. Alarmed by their furtive manner, he knotted the shirt to keep the mangos safe and turned to leave. Two men blocked his path. A scrawny, balding, pinch-faced fellow dressed in a skirt woven of vines and leaves, his tanned body speckled with inflamed mosquito bites, shook a fist at George and said, "Them's our mangos!" Grime deepened the lines on his face, adding a sinister emphasis to his scowl.

His companion was a plump young man with unkempt, shoulder-length hair and a brow as broad and unwritten on as a newly cut tombstone—his head was rather large and his features small and unremarkable, imbuing his face with a weak, unfinished quality. He wore the remnants of corduroy trousers and carried a stick stout enough to be used as a club, but hid it behind his leg and refused to meet George's stare, the very image of a reluctant warrior. George decided the men posed no threat, yet he kept an eye on the figures hiding in the brush.

"I've only taken a dozen or so," he said. "Surely there's enough for everyone."

The balding man adopted an expression that might have been an attempt at ferocity, but instead gave the impression that he suffered from a sour stomach. The plump man whispered to him and he made a disagreeable noise.

"We're camped a long way from here—I hate to return empty-handed," said George. "Let me pass. I won't bother you again."

The plump man looked to his friend and after brief consideration the balding man said, "We can spare a few, I reckon. I apologize for treating you rude, but we've had problems with our neighbors poaching our supplies."

"Neighbors? Is there a village nearby?"

"Naw, just people like us. And you. People what Griaule chased onto the plain. Maybe fifty or sixty of 'em. It's hard to say exactly because most keep to themselves and they're scattered all over. Might be more."

George hefted his mangos, slung them over his shoulder. "Griaule, you say? You're talking about that smallish dragon?"

"Same as chased you out here," said the man. "Quite different from the Griaule we're used to, he is. But you can see it's him if you looks close."

"How long have you been out here?" George asked.

"Three months, a piece more. At least that's how long me and the family's been here." He gestured at the plump man. "Edgar joined us a week or so later."

Edgar grinned at George and nodded.

"Is that your family?" George pointed to the figures in the brush. "Please assure them I mean no harm."

"I'm sure they know that, sir. It's obvious you're a gentleman." The balding man toed the dirt, as if embarrassed. "My daughter took a terrible fright, what with all Griaule's bellowing. She's never been right in the head. Now she ain't comfortable around people....except for Edgar here." Resentment, or something akin, seeped into his voice. "She fair dotes on him."

"How many people are with you, Mister?" asked Edgar, startling George, who had begun to think he was a mute.

"Just a friend and I."

He introduced himself and learned that the balding man was Peter Snelling, his wife was named Sandra and his daughter Peony. These formalities concluded, he asked what use they thought the dragon had for them.

"Might as well ask how much the moon weighs," said Edgar, and Snelling chimed in, "You'll get nowhere attempting to divine his purposes."

"You must have had some thoughts on the subject," said George.

"Don't reckon he wants to eat us," Snelling said. "He wouldn't go to all this trouble...yet he did eat that one fellow."

"Didn't really eat him." Edgar scratched a jowl. "Chewed on him and spit him out is all."

"That was because he tried to run off," said Snelling. "It were Griaule's way of telling the rest of us to stay put."

The idea that anyone could undergo this trial and not expend a great deal of energy in trying to comprehend it was alien to George. In his opinion, it did not speak highly of the two men's intellect. He asked how they had wound up in this desolate place to begin with. Had they, like him, been transported by a magical agency?

"You'd have to talk to Peony," Snelling said. "She were fooling around with something, but she wouldn't show me what it was. Then the walls of our house vanished and there we were, with nothing but nature around us. Peony let out a screech and flung the thing in her hand away. I suppose I should have searched for it." He hunched his shoulders and made a rueful face. "It was hard to swallow, you know, that she were the one responsible. But I'm sure now it was her doing."

"Even if you had found it, it wouldn't have done you much good," said George.

Edgar's eyes darted to the side and George followed his gaze. An immensely fat woman with gray tangles of hair framing a lumpish, sunburned face and wearing a tent-sized piece of canvas for a dress, rushed at him, swinging a tree branch. The branch struck him on the neck and shoulder. Twigs scratched his face; sprays of leaves impaired his vision—a confusing blow yet not that concussive. He staggered to the side, but did not fall. Snelling threw himself on him, riding him piggy-back, and as husband and wife sought to wrestle him to the ground, Edgar poke him with his stick, more annoyance than threat, his moony face bobbing now and then into sight. George managed to shove the woman away and, when she came at him again, he planted a foot in the pit of her stomach, sending her waddling backwards across the clearing, her arms making circular motions as if attempting to fly out of danger. She made a cawing noise and toppled into a bush—her dress rode up around her hips, leaving the raddled flesh of her legs protruding from the leaves. Snelling clung to him, biting and clawing, until George grabbed him by the hair and punched him in the mouth. Edgar dropped his stick, retreated to the edge of the clearing, and stood wringing his hands, his expression shifting from pained to vacant, and finally lapsing into the feckless grin that George took to be the natural resolution of his features.

He wiped blood from his chin, where a twig had nicked him. Snelling lay on his side, breathing through his mouth, blood crimsoning his teeth. His wife struggled to sit up, teetered for a moment, flirting with the perpendicular before falling back again.

"Sandra!" Snelling's cry sounded forlorn, almost wistful, not like a shout of warning, or even one of sympathy.

"Are you mad?" George kicked dirt on him and scooped up his shirt, along with the mangos it held. "Risking your lives for a few mangos! Fucking idiots!"

A noise behind him—he spun about, ready to defend himself. Standing at the margin of the clearing was a gangly young girl in deplorable condition, twelve or thirteen years old. Ginger hair hung across her face in thick snarls and her faded blue rag of a dress did little to hide her immature breasts. In addition to a freckling of inflamed insect bites, the skin of her torso and legs was striped with welts, some of them fresh, evidence of harsh usage. Her lips trembled and she tottered forward. "Help me," she said in a frail voice. She stumbled and might have fallen had George not caught her. She was so slight, when he put an arm about her, he inadvertently lifted her off the ground.

Snelling collapsed onto his back, breath shuddering, but his wife, displaying renewed vigor, shrilled, "Take your hands off my daughter!"

Edgar, displaying unexpected ferocity, charged George with arms outstretched and fingers hooked, as if intending to scratch out his eyes. George stepped to the side and, using the mangos knotted in his shirt, clubbed him in the face. Edgar dropped like a stone, blood spurting from his nose, and began to sob. Between the sobs, George heard Peony speaking almost inaudibly, saying, "She's not my mother…she's not my mother."

"Liar!" Mrs. Snelling shrieked. "Ingrate!"

"She may be your daughter, but you most certainly are not her mother," George said. "No real mother would allow her child to endure such abuse."

"Bastard! If we were in Morningshade, I'd have you beaten."

"Lucky for me we're not in Morningshade. And lucky for you I'm less concerned with justice than I am with caring for your daughter's injuries." George's outrage crested. "My God! What sort of people are you to treat a child so? Wild animals would show more humanity! I'm taking her with me. If you attempt to interfere in any way, I'll finish what I've begun. I'll kill you all!"

To illustrate this message, George kicked Edgar in the thigh. He backed from the clearing and, once he could no longer see them, he picked up Peony and ran.

HE HAD GONE no more than twenty-five yards when a blast of sound assailed him, seeming to come from on high, followed by a windy rush. Glancing up, he glimpsed a pale swollen belly and a twitching serpentine tail passing overhead. Moments later, the bushes crunched under an enormous weight and a low grumbling signaled that Griaule had landed nearby and was crashing through the thickets. George flung himself down, burrowed under the dead fronds scattered beneath a palmetto tree, and gathered Peony to him, clamping a hand to her mouth to prevent an outcry. More crunching, dry twigs snapping like strings of firecrackers; then the great glutinous huff of the dragon breathing. Through a gap in the leaves George saw a thick scaly leg that terminated in a foot as broad as a sofa cushion, with a spike protruding from its heel and four yellowish talons, much discolored. Peony, who had been squirming about, went limp in his arms, and a cold sensation settled over his brain. Cold and seething, like the margins of a tide. He had the impression of an ego gone wormy with age and anger, a malefic, indulgent potency whose whims dwarfed his deepest desires, an entity to which he was intrinsically subservient. A message resolved from the coldness, clear as the reverberations of a gong, silencing every other mental voice, and he knew, as surely as he might know the worn portrait of an empress on a Roman sesturcius, that his place was beside the pools, that he should never return to the mango tree. Such behavior would not be tolerated a second time. He shut his eyes, terror-struck by this brush with Griaule's mind (it had been too alien and powerful to write off as imagination born of fear), and he refused to open them again until he heard leathery wings battering the air and a scream issuing from above the plain.

As THEY MADE their way toward home, he rejected all interior conversation concerning the possibility that the dragon had spoken to him, (though he was certain it had), and he stuffed any material relating to the encounter into his mental attic and locked it away. Denial was the only rational course in the face of such power. To distract himself further, he poked around in the fume and bubble of his thoughts, hoping to learn what had provoked him to such a rage against the Snellings. Not since his schoolboy days had he lifted a hand in anger and, while he had acted in self-defense, the murderous character of the emotions that had attended his actions astonished him. He could not unearth any inciting event from his past that would have predisposed him to such a vicious reaction, yet he realized he had tapped into a res-ervoir of ferocity that must have been simmering inside him for years, waiting a proper outlet. His threats had not been empty bluster. He meant every word.

CHAPTER
FIVE

PEONY WAS TOO WEAK to manage a hike and George had to carry her much of the way. When he questioned her about the Snellings, she put her head down on his shoulder and slept, her heart beating against his chest, frail and rapid as a bird's. With every step, her vulnerability impressed itself on him and his commitment to her deepened. He stopped now and then, hiding in the thickets, waiting until certain no one was trailing them before moving on, and before they reached camp in early afternoon he had reversed the basic situation in his mind and thought about Peony in terms such as might befit a protective parent.

Sylvia was fishing, crouched half-naked in the pool, wearing only her rolled-up trousers. She pretended not to hear his approach. He called out to her and she turned on him a look of exasperation that changed to one of displeasure when she caught sight of Peony.

"Adding to your stable?" she said nastily. "One woman's not enough for a man of your dimensions?"

"Use your eyes," he replied. "She's hardly a woman."

He explained what had occurred and she had him carry Peony inside the shelter, then shooed him away, saying she would tend to the girl.

Five good-sized fish lay on flat stones by the edge of the pool, their glistening sides pulsing with last breaths. One had silvery tiger-stripes on its olive green back—George couldn't identify it. He sliced off their heads, gutted and filleted them, and wrapped their flesh in banana leaves. That done, he took a stroll into the thickets, located a banderilla tree growing beside a cluster of hibiscus bushes, and began removing the barbs from the tips of the twigs, placing them on banana leaves and carrying the leaves to the perimeter of the camp. He was loading his ninth leaf when Sylvia pushed through the bushes to his side and asked what he was doing.

"I'm going to rig some booby traps along the trails," he said. "They won't do serious damage, but we'll hear when someone trips them."

She said nothing, watching him work.

"Is Peony sleeping?" he asked.

She nodded and knelt beside him. "She's going to require a lot of care. I'll do what I can, but...I don't know."

"What's wrong?"

Sylvia shook her head.

"Tell me," George insisted.

"It's what happens to beautiful young girls when there's no one to care for them."

Recalling the way Peony had looked, it was difficult to think of her as beautiful. "What do you mean?"

"Men. As best I can tell, they've been at her since she was eight."

Sylvia's voice quavered with emotion and George suspected that her empathy for the girl might be due to a similarity of experience.

"Men did most of the damage," she said. "But her mother used her as well."

George had the impulse to suggest that being sexually abused by one's mother would have a momentous effect. A centipede crawled onto his ankle—he flicked it off. "Did she say whether the Snellings were her parents?"

"I asked, but she's not clear about it. She's hazy about most things. It's good you brought her here." She uprooted a weed. "I'm sorry for earlier...what I said about you."

"It's all right."

"I had no business saying it. You've treated me better than most." She paused. "She saw Griaule's scale in your kit. I let her keep it, if that suits you."

"That's up to you. It's yours, after all."

After a pause she said, "Could you sleep somewhere else for a while? Peony's grateful for what you did, but it would do her a world of good not to sleep at close quarters with a man."

George mulled this over. "I should build a larger shelter, anyway. We could be here for a while. There's a nice spot by one of the smaller ponds. If I put it there, that should give her enough privacy."

"Thank you."

"Once I finish with the booby traps, I'll get started."

She made as if to stand, but held in a crouch with one hand flat to the ground, and then settled back onto her knees. "One more thing. Can I have your shirt? I want to cut it up and make her a halter."

"There's no need to cut it up. It'll be too big for her, but it'll do the job."

"I thought I might make something for myself to wear, too. I know you like watching my titties, but they're an encumbrance for me."

He heard resentment in her tone, but her face remained neutral.

"You were using it as a carry-all," she said. "I don't figure you'll miss it so much."

He shrugged out of the shirt and handed it to her. "I'd give it a wash first."

She stood, holding the shirt in both hands. Again he thought she might speak and when she did not he lowered his head and went to twisting banderilla barbs from the twigs.

"Save me a fish," he said.

CHAPTER SIX

ORN OUT BY HIS labors, by emotional tumult, George fell asleep in the partially completed new shelter shortly after dark. He was overtired and slept fitfully, now and again waking to a twinge of strained muscles, conscious of scudding dark clouds that obscured all but thin seams of stars, and of wind rattling the palm thatch, raising a susurrus from the surrounding thickets. During such an interlude a shadow slipped inside the shelter and lay next to him, her fingers spidering across his belly and his groin. He intended to tell her that he was too tired, too sore, but while he was still half-asleep, his senses pleasantly muddled, she took him in her mouth, her tongue doing clever things, finishing him quickly, and then she slipped from the shelter and was gone, leaving him with the impression that the wind and the darkness had conspired to produce a lover whose sensuality was the warm, breathing analogue of the rustling thatch and the sighing thickets. Waking late the next morning, he half-believed it had been a dream or a visitation of some sort until he saw Sylvia beside the pool and she flashed a smile that persuaded him the intimacy had neither been imagined nor supernatural in origin.

Peony stood by her on the bank, but on spotting George she stepped behind Sylvia as if anxious. He would not have recognized her in a different context, though the marks of abuse were more prominent now that her skin was clean. Her hair was pulled back from her face, exposing high cheekbones and huge cornflower blue eyes and a mouth too wide for her delicate jaw and pointed chin. It was a face of such otherworldly beauty, George's initial glimpse of it affected him like a slap and he felt a measure of alarm. Both Peony and Sylvia wore halters fashioned from his shirt and, while they did not much resemble one another, this made them seem like a mother and daughter—he doubted Sylvia was older than twenty-two or twenty-three, yet she possessed a maturity that lent her a maternal aspect when compared with Peony. George found appealing the notion that the three of them might constitute a family.

"I'm George," he said to Peony. "Do you remember me?"

Peony had been peering at him over Sylvia's shoulder, but now she looked away, showing him her left profile.

"How are you feeling?" he asked.

She kept her eyes averted. "I'm afraid."

"You needn't be afraid. The people who hurt you…"

"It's not them she's afraid of," Sylvia said. "It's Griaule."

"He wants to show me something," Peony said. "But I won't look."

George rubbed at an ache in his shoulder. "I don't understand."

"We'll be fine." Sylvia fixed him with a stare, as if daring him to object. "Peony will be safe here, won't she?"

"Oh, yes. Absolutely." He continued to rub his shoulder and asked Peony how she knew Griaule's mind.

"It's not so clear with the scale Sylvia gave me," Peony said. "Mine was better. But…"

George waited for her to go on. She fingered the ends of her hair and did not speak.

"What's not so clear?" he asked.

"It's like he's whispering to me, but there's no voice."

"You hear him talking? He talks to you?"

"He wants me to look at something awful," she said. "He wants us all to look."

"Do you ever hear him without touching the scale? After I took you from the Snellings, did you hear him then?"

She shot George a quizzical look. "Lots of people hear him when he's angry."

"Do you think the Snellings heard him?"

"I've got to get to my fishing. The later the hour, the harder they are to catch." Sylvia went to one knee and began rolling up a pants leg. "If you two could look after each other, maybe gather some fruit, that would be nice."

George frowned. "I was going to collect some saplings I can use for poles. You know, for the shelter."

"Is there a reason you can't take her with you?" Sylvia came to her feet and said under her breath, "I need time to myself." She nodded at Peony and grimaced, as if to imply the girl was a trial, and then, in a normal voice: "See if you can bring back some grapes. I'm told there used to be grapevines out here."

"Grapes!" Peony's giggle seemed edged with dementia.

"Yes," said Sylvia. "What about them?"

"You might as well eat eyes. That's what Edgar says."

"Edgar?"

"The man living with her parents," said George.

"They don't taste like eyes," Peony said. "But they're squishy like eyes."

"How does he know?" Sylvia asked her. "Is Edgar an eye-eater? Does he relish a nice eye on occasion? Does he dip 'em in melted butter and let 'em slide down his gullet?"

Peony appeared to struggle with the question; her expression lost its sharpness and her gaze wandered.

"I'll wager he's an eye-eater," Sylvia said. "Most men are."

THAT CONVERSATION, GEORGE discovered, was Peony at her most coherent. Much of the time she was unresponsive, even when asked a direct question, and she would hum or sing in her pale voice, fiddling with a leaf or a pebble, whatever fell to hand. Nevertheless he managed to piece together a vision of her life with Edgar and the Snellings. She declined to talk about Sandra—her face tightened each time George broached the subject—but said that Mr. Snelling had been in the habit of grabbing her whenever Sandra chose not to perform her wifely duty; he would turn Peony "bottoms up" and beat her for her lack of enthusiasm. Edgar had weaseled his way into her affections, pretending to be a friend, and cajoled her into using her mouth to soothe him after a hard day of eating mangos. His fondness for a sexual practices associated with sailors on long voyages had alienated Peony, yet she spoke of him fondly in contrast to her remarks about the Snellings. Having learned all this, George reserved the majority of his loathing for Edgar. Younger and stronger than the Snellings, he might have assisted Peony, but chose instead to gratify his lust, helping transform her into this broken thing.

Thenceforth George cared for Peony from the time he woke until late afternoon, at which point Sylvia took charge. He dragged her along whenever he searched for edibles (feeding three people occupied most of their day and though they went about it with diligence, they lost weight and strength at a startling rate). As a consequence, he and Sylvia were rarely alone together. It was hardly the family life he had envisioned, yet it was not dissimilar to the life he and Rosemary had shared, albeit with greater responsibilities and less frequent sex. Sylvia had not visited him in the new shelter since the night after he had returned with Peony. He believed on that occasion she must have been grateful for his intercession on Peony's behalf, and he told himself that in order to obtain sexual favors on a regular basis he might have to save other young women from exigent circumstances. He was tempted to coerce her by saying that he needed this consolation, that the strain of days spent worrying and watching out for the dragon was taking its toll (it would not have been an outright lie—his waking hours were marked by depressive fugues). Then seventeen days after Peony had entered their lives, Sylvia visited him again, crawling into the shelter as he was falling asleep.

A three-quarter moon shone into the shelter, gilding their bed of banana leaves, and when Sylvia mounted him she became a silhouette limned in golden light, her hair tossing about like black flames, an impression supported by the thatch crackling in the wind. She was eager and enthusiastic as never before, and George, fancying this increase signaled more than mere animal intensity, responded with enthusiasm. Afterward, however, she broke the post-coital silence by saying, "I don't want you taking this personal. I had an itch I couldn't scratch, you understand."

"Why would I suppose otherwise?"

Moonlight erased the marks of strain on her face and she seemed a younger, less troubled version of herself. "Because I know how men get," she said.

George scoffed at this. "They're such primitive creatures, aren't they? Quick to arouse and to anger. Otherwise they're like backward children."

"About some things they are. Do you think I'm such a ninny, I can't tell your feelings are hurt? I'm sorry, but I don't want you to come away with the wrong idea."

"Let me assure you, I know exactly where we stand."

Another silence stretched between them, and then George said, "One thing is puzzling. You told me intercourse was out of the question because you didn't have your 'medicines'."

"Peony says we won't be here long. If you get me in a family way, I'll fix it when we return to Teocinte."

"You believe her? You'd take the word of a child who'd stare into the sun all day if we allowed it?"

"I've had to accept greater improbabilities. I've accepted that you brought us to this place by rubbing a dragon's scale. People like Peony are often compensated for their impairment with a gift. But who..."

"Don't tell me you put any stock in that old business!"

"Who'd imagine a solid citizen like yourself would be so blessed?"

"Is that an insult in your view? Calling me a solid citizen?"

"I didn't mean it as such, but if that's how you choose to interpret it."

"I suppose 'solid citizen' must seem an insult to..." George bit back the last of his sentence.

"A whore? Is that the word you want?"

"We're trapped in this situation. It's pointless to fight."

"Pointless it may be, but I..."

"Stop it!" he said, wrapping his arms about her and drawing her close, so that they were pressed chest-to-chest. "We've greater troubles to deal with. And greater enemies."

"Let me go!"

She sought to wriggle free, but he held her tightly. She pulled away from him as far as his grip permitted, as if to gain a fresh perspective, and asked, "What do you want?"

"Just that we try to get along."

"This..." Although under restraint, she succeeded in conveying that she was speaking of their closeness. "This isn't getting along?"

"You know what I mean."

"We share the work, we each do our part in taking care of Peony. What else is there?"

"You could be pleasant."

"Ah! You want me to pretend."

"No! I want you to be like you were at the hotel. You remember. When you asked if I liked you when you weren't pretending to be someone else."

Amused, she said, "You don't believe I was pretending then?"

He tamped down his anger. "I don't care what you were doing, only that you do more of it. In spite of your faith in Peony's clairvoyance, it could be months or years before we find our way home. We could be stuck here the rest of our lives. We need to make a better effort at getting along or we'll drive each other mad."

"We don't have to get along. We're not married."

"Is that right? We bicker constantly, we have sex infrequently and we're responsible for a child. That sounds like a marriage to me. Unlike a marriage, however, we can't escape its context by having a night out. Whatever you were doing, pretending, not pretending, it might be helpful if you started doing it again. Neither of us is a trusting person, but we have to trust one another. We have no idea what's going on and we may have to depend on each other more than we do now. We need to develop a bond. If we can't, we have no chance of surviving."

"Are you finished?"

"Yes, I suppose I am."

"Let me go."

With a frustrated noise, he pushed her away and she rolled up to her knees. Curls and flecks of banana leaf were stuck to the sweat on her hip and thigh—they might have been the remnants of script, as if their love-making had written a green sentence on her flesh that their argument had mostly erased. He expected her to bolt without further word, but once she regained her footing she stood with her head down, hair hanging in her face, her fingers intertwined at her waist.

"Are you all right?" he asked.

She wiped her nose.

"I didn't mean to upset you," he said. "I'm merely suggesting we'd be better off if we were honest with one another. If we make a sincere effort at establishing a relationship, a friendship, then who knows what may develop. If a spark is given sufficient tinder…"

"Don't you ever stop?" She clasped both hands to her head as though to prevent it from exploding. "You get an idea and you go on and fucking on about it! You don't care what anyone else is going through so long as you hear the sound of your voice." She sniffled, wiped her nose again, and squared her shoulders. "I'm sorry. I truly am."

With that, she hurried off into the darkness, leaving George to contemplate the error of his ways, to puzzle over her apology and to listen to the wind intoning its ceaseless consonant-less sentence, like a mantra invoking an idiot god.

✠

Judging by the way their conversation ended, George did not expect a happy result; but the upshot of the encounter was that Sylvia began coming to him every few nights, and they would make love and discuss practical considerations, most having to do with Peony. They were, he reflected, becoming if not a traditional family, then a functional one. He suspected that Sylvia's heart was not in the relationship, but her pretence pleased him, nourishing a longstanding fantasy and sustaining him against the two oppressive, unvarying presences that ruled over the plain: the heat and the dragon. At times he was unable to distinguish between them—the dragon patrolling overhead seemed emblematic of the terrible heat, and the heat seemed the enfeebling by-product of the dragon's mystery and menace. Without Sylvia's affections and his paternal regard for Peony, he might have succumbed to depression. The days played out with unrelenting sameness: too-bright mornings and oven-like noons giving way to skies with low gray clouds sliding past, their bellies dark with rain that never fell, and a damp closeness turning the air to soup—it was as if they were living in the humid mouth of a vast creature too large to apprehend, one of which they had only unpleasant and unreliable intimations. Of course the dragon was the most salient threat, the one for which there was neither explanation nor remedy. Though he had denigrated

Edgar and Snelling for their lack of interest in the question, George soon realized that any attempted analysis relating to the dragon's purposes would be pure speculation. The most sensible explanation he came up with was that the dragon was using the plain as storehouse for its food supply, but this raised other questions, notably why would Griaule bother to choose its human treats by so indirect a procedure (assuming the others had been transported to the plain by touching or rubbing immature dragon scales). He inquired of Peony again, asking what she knew of Griaule's designs, but she spoke in generalities, repeating her original statement that he wanted them to witness something, adding to this that they were "the lucky ones." When he pressed her, she grew tearful and mumbled something about "fire."

✠

GEORGE HAD NOT entirely accepted that the dragon of the moment was Griaule, or that, as this would imply, Griaule was still alive, and he found Peony's failure to resolve the question unbearably frustrating. He tried every means of coercion at his disposal, but nothing caused her to elaborate on the subject and he decided that the only thing to do was to table the matter. To occupy his mind, he began teaching Peony about the natural world, lessons she did not appear capable of absorbing. As they wandered the plain in their never-ending search for food, he would point out the various trees and

bushes and repeat their names, and he explained processes like the sunrise and rain, often over-explaining
them, a tactic that may have annoyed Sylvia but to which
Peony raised no objection.

One day while they were exploring the thickets to the
west of the stream, they happened upon a kumquat tree
that had escaped the attention of the birds, its boughs
laden with dusky orange fruit. George sat beneath it and
fashioned a makeshift basket out of banana leaves, while
Peony nibbled at the fruit, gnawing away the flesh from
around the big brown pits. After she had consumed over
a dozen kumquats he told her that if she didn't stop she
might experience stomach trouble. She plucked another
kumquat. He repeated his warning to no effect and finally
snapped at her, forbidding her to eat more—she dropped
the kumquat and refused to look at him. He patted her
on the arm, feeling like a bully, and lectured her in detail
on the consequences of eating too much fruit.

As the sun approached its zenith, George located a
patch of shade large enough to shelter them and stretched
out for a nap with Peony beside him. He emerged from
an erotic dream to find that Peony had unbuttoned the
remnants of his trousers and was fondling him. At first
he thought it part of the dream, but then he pushed her
away. She made a pleading sound and tried once more
to fondle him—he shouted at her to quit and she cov-
ered her head with her hands, as if to shield herself from
a blow.

"You mustn't do that," he said. "You don't have to do that anymore. No one will hurt you if you don't."

She met his eyes without the least sign of comprehension; a tear cut a track though a spot of grime on her cheek.

"It's all right," he said. "I'm not angry at you. I'm angry at the people who taught you this was how you should please them."

She gazed at him blankly, her face empty as a fresh-washed bowl embossed with an exotic pattern. She drew a wavy line in the dirt with a fingertip and looked at him again.

"Do you understand?" he said. "You never have to do this anymore. Not with anyone."

A worry line creased her brow. "I want to make people happy."

"Where this is concerned, touching people, allowing them to touch you…the important thing is to please yourself."

She made a clumsy pawing gesture and lowered her eyes; she saw the kumquat she had let fall and reached for it, then pulled back her hand.

"From now on," he said, "if you have the urge to make anyone happy that way, if anyone asks you to make them happy, you come to me and ask what to do. Or ask Sylvia. Will you do that?"

She nodded and reached for the kumquat. He started again to reproach her, but decided that she had enough to think about.

It was not until after he handed her off to Sylvia that he began to speculate about his hesitation in pushing Peony away, thinking his reflexes may have been slowed not by sleep as much as by perversity; and it was not until that evening that he began to wonder about that first night after he had rescued Peony, when Sylvia had come to him...if it had been Sylvia. Her touch seemed in memory less practiced, less confident, akin to Peony's in that regard. And surely Silvia would have spoken to him—it was not like her to be so shy. The longer he thought about it, the greater his certitude that Peony had expressed gratitude the only way she knew. The idea repelled him yet he could not stop dwelling on it. As he went over the events of that night, a measure of prurience crept into his thoughts, repelling him further. He hewed to the notion that this was how the obsessive mind worked, seeking ever to betray itself, subverting every clean impulse by assigning it a base motive; yet as the days wore on he insisted upon punishing himself for his crimes. Even when occupied by the basics of survival, part of him was always focused upon Peony, upon what he had or hadn't done.

The matter should have been easy to resolve, but when Sylvia next visited him, George had feared that anything she said about that night would support his self-imposed verdict. Better, he decided, to maintain a modicum of doubt concerning his moral turpitude than to have none. He was unable to perform with Sylvia, excusing his failure by claiming to have stomach trouble, and as they lay listening to the wind flowing across the plain, watching clouds skimming a half-moon that set their edges on silvery fire, he allowed this intimacy to change his mind and blurted out what had happened between him and Peony the day before, and asked Sylvia if she had come to him the night following the rescue, because he feared now that it had not been her.

She was silent for a beat and then turned to face him. "Is that what's got you in a twist? Of course it was me!" She gave him a playful punch. "I'm insulted you didn't recognize me!"

Later he realized that if he had desired an honest response, he would have asked the question without preamble, not letting on that he suspected his visitor had been Peony, telling Sylvia that he'd had a dream and he wondered whether or nor it was real. He should never have afforded her the opportunity to weigh the situation, to determine that it would be best for her if she lied, thus giving his confidence a boost and assuring that he would remain capable of defending her. This scenario called for a complex understanding on her part, but he had long since discarded the idea that she was other than an intelligent, subtle woman. And so the conflict remained unresolved, continuing to erode his mental underpinnings, distracting him from more important considerations.

George could not separate himself from Peony during the day, but he minimized their physical contact and treated her with a rigid formality, permitting neither hugs nor holding hands. That the loss of a simple animal comfort appeared to have no effect on her should have offered him a degree of absolution, since it pointed out how damaged she was, how trivial an influence the actions of others had upon her inner turmoil; but instead it served to distress him further, seeming to add to his offense, and made him even more mindful of her well-being than he had been before. Every scraped knee and pricked finger was cause for worry; every complaining noise engaged his full concern. When he was unable to sleep (something that happened with increasing frequency), in order to safeguard her more thoroughly he would patrol the perimeter of the camp with a regularity that rivaled the dragon's, taking pains to avoid his own booby traps. One evening as he made his rounds, he heard a succession of cries coming from the thickets out past his shelter. They subsided as he approached and he could hear nothing except the wind. An oblate moon emerged from cloud cover to the south, silvering the fluttering tops of the bushes and showing his path. Soon he heard the voices again. Men's querulous voices. He crept toward the sound, peeking between leaves. Separated from the bank of one of the lesser pools by a thin fringe of vegetation, two men sat athwart an animal trail. Delicate rills of blood, black in the moonlight, trickled from wounds on their legs—they had fallen into one of his traps and were picking out banderilla barbs from their flesh. The smaller of the two, a sinewy man with a mane of dark hair half-hiding his face, wearing a pair of rotting trousers, cursed as he removed a barb, digging at his calf with the tip of fishing knife. The other man was Edgar. He had received fewer injuries and was cautious with the barbs, yipping as he worked them free.

Anger flowed into George's mind, like a rider swinging with practiced ease onto his mount—it was as if he'd been preparing for this moment for weeks and, now it had arrived, he was more than ready to perform whatever duties were required. He stepped onto the trail, but before he could speak the sinewy man sprang to his feet, and made an awkward, hobbling lunge toward George and slashed with the knife, drawing a line of hot pain across his abdomen. A second stroke sliced his forearm. Panicking, George flung himself forward and grappled with the man, locking onto the wrist of his knife-hand. They swayed together like drunken dancers and careened through the bushes and out onto the bank. His opponent was strong, but George, much the larger of the two, had leverage on his side—he turned the man and secured a hold from behind and rode him down onto his knees at the brink of the pool. The knife went skittering along the bank and, as the man sought to retrieve it, George moved atop him, using his weight to flatten him out, and forced his head underwater. He surfaced and twisted his neck about, offering a view of his grizzled cheek, grimacing mouth and a mad, glaring eye that glittered through a webbing of wet hair. His fetid odor enveloped them both. He grunted and gulped in air; then his head went under again and his struggles grew spastic, frantic, churning the water. He reached back with his left hand, trying to claw George's face, and George latched his fingers behind the man's neck and pushed down harder, his eyes fixed on the opposite side of the pool. He spotted Sylvia in a half-crouch at the verge of the bushes, but took no salient notice of her. Spasms passed through the man's flesh, lewd convulsions like those of a lover nearing completion. George kept pushing down on his neck, making sure. Finally he rolled off the body and lay panting beside it. The moonlight had brightened. His stomach throbbed. He sat up to inspect the wound: it appeared superficial. The cut on his forearm was more worrisome. If the man hadn't been impeded by injuries, George thought, then he might be the one who lay motionless. His hands shook. A placid current set the dead man's head to bobbing. George imagined fish nibbling at the eyes and thought to pull the body from the water, but wasn't moved to act. The smell of the man was on his skin, nauseatingly thick. Sylvia kneeled beside him, saying words he couldn't make sense of. The sight of her confused him on a fundamental level, disordered all his certainties. He wanted to look away, but her insistent stare held him. She spoke again, her tone fretful, and he said, "I'm all right."

She slapped him. "The other one's getting away!"

He cast about, but saw no one.

"Here!" She pressed the dead man's knife into his hand, its blade frilled with red. Resting on his palm, it had an incomprehensible value.

"It's only Edgar," he said.

"Edgar? The one who was holding Peony captive? And that..." She gestured at the body. "That was Snelling?"

"I don't know who he was." George set the knife down on the grass. "But Edgar's no threat. He's harmless on his own."

"But he wasn't on his own, was he? He must have talked his friend into having a little adventure. Told him there was a nice piece over this way and suggested they fetch her back. Do you call that harmless?" She left a pause and, when he kept silent, she said, "If you won't do something, I will."

She snatched at the knife, but George closed his hand on the hilt and creakily came to his feet, feeling light-headed and feverish, moved not by an urge to seek out Edgar, but by the desire to stop her talking.

Edgar was not difficult to track. After they had walked the trail for several minutes, George heard a voice nattering on at a conversational volume. Thirty feet farther along they reached a creosote bush—many of its leaves were stripped away and it threw a complicated shadow across the ground—Edgar sat at the center of this shadow, like an innocent young demon with a moony face summoned by a magical design. He picked at a spine in his heel, noticed them and grinned sheepishly, as if he had been caught at something naughty.

"I told you, didn't I?" he said, apparently addressing himself. "Leave 'em alone, I said."

George hunkered down in front of him. "Where are the Snellings?"

Edgar was thinner than before, his cheeks hollowed, his belly flab reduced. He nodded, as if listening to an invisible someone responding to his chiding. George yelled at him to gain his attention and repeated his inquiry.

"Peter's dead," Edgar said. "And Sandra's took ill. That's why me and Tony come. To see if you had medicine."

Sylvia made a disparaging noise.

"If that was your purpose," George said, "why did Tony try to kill me?"

Edgar puzzled over this. "I reckon because you surprised him. He didn't know you from Adam."

"You could have said something, couldn't you? You could have told him who I was."

He fingered his ratty hair. "I reckon you surprised me, too."

"Finish this," Sylvia said flatly.

"I want to ask him some more questions," said George.

"He's making things up as he goes along. It's obvious!"

George spoke to Edgar. "You wanted to see Peony, didn't you?"

"I'm always wanting to see Peony, but that weren't why we come."

"Did you tell Tony about her?"

Edgar's mouth worked, as if tasting some sourness. "I don't recall."

Sylvia threw up her hands. "Can't we have done with this?"

George stood and pulled her aside, out of Edgar's hearing. "Lying or not, he can't harm us. He's simple."

"You say he's simple, I say it's an act. But be that as it may, suppose another Tony happens along—do you think he won't tell him about Peony? He wants her back, can't you see that?"

"We survived Tony, we'll survive the next one."

"We barely survived! You may be willing to put yourself at risk for no good reason, but not me."

George glanced at Edgar—he was picking at his heel.

"This is the man you blamed for Peony's condition," said Sylvia. "I'm not wrong about that, am I?"

"I think we need to step back a moment," George said. "We don't always have to react straightaway."

"You great fucking idiot!" Sylvia looked as though she wanted to spit. "All this time out here, after everything we've been through, and you still don't know who you are...or where you are. You just killed a man in self-defense. Held him under the water until his lungs burst because he threatened us. Now you're reluctant to finish the job. I guess you'd rather pretend you're a moral sort. That you're too sensitive to be a killer. You need time to contemplate the idea, to fit it into your philosophy of life. Well, maybe that'll make you feel better, but feeling better won't change the fact that there's no place for morality here. If truth be told, there's no place for it in Morningshade, either. Nor anywhere, really."

"You're being ridiculous. I keep telling you Edgar's not a threat."

"Everyone's a threat! There's no law here except Griaule's. If he wasn't flying around all hours, frightening everybody, people would be braver, they'd explore their surroundings. And if that were the case, like as not Peony and I would be slaving away on our backs day and night, and you'd be dead. We're fortunate the people camped close to us were cowards." She prodded his chest with a finger. "Sooner or later Edgar's bound to tell his story to someone more adept at killing than you. Someone who's not hampered by morality. Then we'll find out how moral you are."

Edgar started to mumble. The wind tailed off—George could hear the rush of the stream. The sound fatigued him and filled him with melancholy.

"You want him dead?" He offered her the knife. "I've shed enough blood this evening."

Her face closed down, armored by a blank expression. George expected her to back away from his challenge, but after a pause, as he was about to say, "What are you waiting for?", she seized the knife and went toward Edgar with a decisive step. At the last instant he turned his head, grinning at her, and she drove the knife into the side of his neck, giving a truncated cry as she struck. The force of the blow knocked Edgar onto his side, tearing the hilt from her grasp, and she fell back, as if shocked by the result. He made a mewling noise and pressed his fingers to the steel protruding from his neck; dark blood jumped between them, spattering his pale shoulder. He seemed to be straining at something, trying to preserve a critical balance, perhaps torn between the desire to yank out the blade and the thought that such an action would be the end of him. His legs kicked out, briefly causing it to appear that he was running in place. Then the straining aspect ebbed from his limbs and he lay staring at the base of the creosote bush. Off in the night, the dragon screamed.

CHAPTER SEVEN

ROM THEN ON, CERTAIN illusions went by the board, the illusion that they were a family foremost among them. George and Sylvia stopped having sex, a decision that was mutual albeit unspoken, and there was an overall diminution of pleasantries; yet these things seemed to indicate a larger change, one whose most profound symptom was an atmosphere of dejection, if not outright defeat. It was as if the spark that gave them life had been dampened. Occasionally that spark sputtered and sparked, providing a bright moment, as on the night when Sylvia told a story she'd written and memorized, one of several she related, all set in Ali's Eternal Reward, concerning a girl of the brothel and her romance with a man who was the spitting image of the

Sinistral from a deck of fortune-telling cards. Peony was entranced by the story and George offered extravagant praise that brought a smile to Sylvia's face; but that flare of good feeling quickly faded and they were as before—three damaged people with no palpable bond to shield them against the oppressions of heaven and the disappointments of the world.

Peony became severely agitated in the week that followed Edgar's death, and, though Sylvia swore Peony had been asleep, George assumed that it was due to her having witnessed Edgar's execution...or perhaps sensed it in some fashion. She would rock on her haunches, fists clenched, making noises like a tiny teakettle, and nothing would console her. After four days she ceased being agitated and instead sat fiddling with the dragon scale, sometimes lapsing into a state that resembled catatonia, drooling and listless and completely unresponsive. Memories and dreams of the man he had killed and of Edgar, the man in whose death he had been complicit, plagued George's nights. He wondered if Sylvia had trouble sleeping, curious as to how efficient her justifications were in protecting her against the depredations of conscience—he suspected they served her very well, indeed. His own sleep was fitful at best. He commonly woke well before sunrise, a circumstance that left him exhausted and slow-brained by day's end, and he would nod off while sitting or even standing. At dusk, ten days after the killings, following a brief lapse

of this sort, he stood at the margin of the camp, looking blearily across the plain, and observed a yellowish
red glow on the horizon beneath a line of slate clouds.
Sunset was his first thought, but then he realized that
he was not facing west and what he had taken for clouds
were actually the peaks of the eastern hills. The glow
issued from an area between the hills and his vantage
point. For a minute he watched it brighten and spread,
thinking it odd. He heard piping cries and saw four or
five people running through the thickets, their heads
visible over the tops of the bushes. The dragon wheeled
above and he assumed they were fleeing him. Fools,
though. The edges of the glow wavered and he thought
he detected a smoky odor. He stared dumbly a moment
before recognizing the source of the glow. The plain was
burning and a brisk wind was driving a wall of flame
toward them.

✠

SHOUTING THE ALARM, he raced to the shelter and found
Sylvia and Peony outside, frightened and clinging together, asking questions with their eyes. He flung out
an arm toward the east and said, "The thickets are
on fire, the wind's bringing it straight for us. We have
to run!"

Light had almost faded from the sky when they
began their westward flight, going at a steady pace, carrying nothing other than the rags on their back and a

few meager possessions, like a family out of prehistory, united in fear. Soon they were racing in full night, yet before long the darkness was illuminated by the fire—they could see the spikes of separate flames and hear a dim roaring. George tried to keep close to the stream, but Griaule harried and herded them in a direction of his choosing. George had little doubt that he had set the plain afire in order to simplify that chore. Now and again the dragon would drop out of the sky, a creature of shadow with scales burnished by flame, and bellow at them, altering their course and adding his fierce noise to the din of the fire. On several occasions they made contact with other groups, but the people never materialized from the darkness sufficiently to identify or count their number. They shied away, as if their time on the plain had acclimated them to fear and suspicion. Hedgerows of fire closed around them. They stumbled and reeled through the thickets, their glistening faces dark with soot, darting this way and that to avoid sudden new channels of flame that threatened to hem them in. Peony fell and George picked her up; when Sylvia began to stagger and her pace faltered, he supported her with his free hand. There was so much smoke in the air, breathing was a chore, and this broke his concentration, causing him to feel fatigue. Griaule harrowed them onward, looming out of the night with his wings half-unfolded, seeming more terrible for being partially visible in the dark, here a reddened fang gleaming, here flame reflected in a golden eye, his roar outvoicing the roar of the flames, snapping, gusting flames that sucked oxygen from the air and heated it so that he felt his throat crack whenever he inhaled. He lost his bearings and suspected that Griaule was toying with them, that he would wear them out and let them to burn in a cul de sac; but he was too weary to come up with an escape plan, too wasted to care, and found himself hoping for a swift resolution, whatever form it might take.

The wind must have changed, because the temperature dropped and the light from the burning plain dimmed, occulted by a mixture of smoke and fog—still the dragon herded them along. They emerged from the thickets onto a grassy slope and, after no more than thirty yards, the slope grew steeper, rockier. Visibility was poor and George had to feel his way—it was as if they were ascending a crag whose lower reaches had the semblance of a crude stair, each step a couple of feet high. He couldn't hear the fire anymore and, though perplexed by this development, he was too enervated to worry. Soon what sounded like muted voices came to his ear. As his eyes adjusted to the darkness he realized that the steps of the stair were very wide and scattered about on them were small groups of people. He steered clear of these and found an unoccupied space where they could sit. The dragon rumbled below, but it was a ruminative sound, or so George chose to interpret it. He was done with running, unable to go another foot.

"Where are we?" Sylvia asked, pressing close for warmth—it had gotten cold and she and Peony sheltered under his arms.

"Don't you know?"

"I thought we were heading back toward Teocinte… where it used to stand. But there's no place like this near the city."

"We'll puzzle it out in the morning," he said. "Get some rest."

George made a manful effort to keep watch, but the gentle breathing of the women seduced him and he fell into a dreamless sleep, waking to discover that the sky had grayed and a dense fog sealed them in against tiers of stone, a kind of amphitheater, perhaps a natural formation[10]. The morning wind picked up, causing eddies and rifts in the fog, revealing sections of the plain—it disquieted

---

10   The amphitheater was not natural, but had been excavated from the side of a hill during Sylvia and George's absence from Teocinte (a term of years, and not of months, as they perceived it), its purpose being to provide seating for audiences who had come to witness a Sound and Light performance. Such a performance never occurred, though the lamps had been set in place and a stage built for the orchestra, and some have conjectured that the impulse to construct the amphitheater came not from the city fathers, as had been thought, but from a more subtle agency whose penchant for such ironies had been noted throughout the long history of Teocinte, and it was also thought that the seating had not been intended for tourists, but for precisely the audience that occupied it on the morning after George, Sylvia and Peony had been forced to flee their encampment.

him to see that the thickets showed yellowish green, not a trace of the previous night's fire, and there was no smell of burning. Every part of his body ached and he would have liked to shake out the kinks and have a look around, as people on the tiers beneath were doing (from what he could tell, there were less than fifty altogether, though he could not be certain, what with the fog); but he wanted to let Peony and Sylvia sleep as long as they could and contented himself with passive observation.

The people clustered on the steps, as sooty and ragged as George, kept an eye on the other groups around them, displaying no inclination to socialize, perhaps focused on the hope that their ordeal might be over, thus having no interest in anything apart from their own preoccupations. That hope, however, did not long persist, for an immense shape began to materialize from the fog directly in front of the amphitheater and, while he had no reason to despair (on the contrary, the vista that opened before him should by its familiarity have relieved his every concern), the sight of Griaule, not his lesser incarnation but the great paralyzed, recumbent beast with his evil snout, his fangs festooned with vines and epiphytes, and scales embroidered with lichen and bird droppings, his greens and golds muted by an overcast, ghost-dressed in streamers of mist, the cavern of his mouth enclosing enough darkness to fill the naves of four or five cathedrals, the hill of his body looming above the tin roofs, the shanty districts and factory precincts of Morningshade from which now arose a clangor of bells…that sight had such a grim, iconic value, like a gigantic conceit enclosing the gates of some abyssal domain, George's strength failed him and the other witnesses appeared similarly afflicted. Their murmurous voices grew silent and they stopped milling about and stood frozen in a dozen separate tableaus. Waking, Peony screamed and buried her face in George's shoulder, and Sylvia drew in a breath sharply and pricked his arm with her fingernails. A chthonic rumbling was heard, so all-encompassing a sound it seemed to issue from the earth, the sky, from the core of all things, as if the basic stuff of matter had gained a voice and were offering complaint, and from Griaule's mouth, in a trickle at first, and then a tide darkening the grass, came the creatures that dwelled within his enormous bulk, slithering, crawling, creeping, flying, hopping, running on four legs and two (for among the snakes and spiders and skizzers and flakes[11] were a number of derelict men and women who, for whatever reason, had sought to shelter inside the dragon, in the hollows and caves and canyons formed by his organs and bones and cartilage). As they fled, dispersing across the plain, the witnesses made out a distant clamor composed of the affrighted cries of the citizens of Morningshade and various alarms

---

11   Parasitic creatures peculiar to Griaule. Skizzers were relatively benign, but flakes, commonly camouflaging themselves as part of a scale, exuded a poison from their skin that led to the deaths of countless unwary scalehunters.

being sounded. Griaule's eyes blinked open, wheels of gold flecked with mineral hues, each divided by a horizontal slit pupil, lending a vile animus to his face. In the depths of his throat bloomed an orange radiance that whitened and shone more fiercely until it resembled a star lodged in his gullet. Seeing this, between ten or fifteen of the witnesses broke from the tiers of the amphitheater and raced toward the town below. Among them was Peony. She shrugged off George's arm, eluded his lunging attempt to snatch her back and scampered down the tiers.

Somewhat reluctantly, Sylvia made to stand, and George said, "It'll be less of a risk if I go alone. Wait for us on the plain. We'll find you."

Relief and shame mixed in her face. "I don't think she knows where she used to live," she said. "Look for her at Griaule's temple. She thought it was pretty inside."

"Where else?"

She shook her head. "I don't know." And then, as he started off, she called, "The brothel! Maybe there! Because of my stories!"

They had been seated near the top tier and George had descended about two-thirds of its height when Griaule, with a coughing grunt that signaled a mighty effort, turned his head and twisted his body in the direction of Haver's Roost, his snout projecting out across the tin roofs—in the same motion, with a tremendous creaking and popping of calcified joints, noises that might have been created by tree trunks snapping, he pushed himself erect, moving with a ponderous, rickety deliberation bred by thousand of years of muscular disuse. It was an unreal sight, a mountainous transformation, the coming-to-life of a colossus. Griaule took a step forward and, with an earthshaking thump, planted a front foot among the shanties of Morningshade, crushing a considerable acreage and all that lived thereon, raising a dust cloud that boiled up around his foreleg, obscuring it. The soil and vegetation surrounding Hangtown, the village on the dragon's back, slid off his side and wings in huge clumps, and the shacks that constituted the village followed, disintegrating in mid-air; from his position, George could not tell where the debris landed. Griaule roared, a blast of raw noise that deafened him[12]. Pain drove him to his knees; he clasped both hands to his ears, squeezed his eyes shut, and when he looked again he saw a gush of flame (patterned with a shifting orange efflorescence that gave it an odd, lacey delicacy) spew from Griaule's mouth and lance across the valley to engulf the hotels on the slopes of Haver's Roost. Within seconds, every building on the Roost, even the government offices atop it, was burning. The dragon appeared to wobble for a instant, but maintained his stance and, lowering and turning his

---

12   The roar killed and injured several thousand people, most of them struck by flying glass from a myriad shattered windows. Nearly half the population suffered damage to their hearing to one degree or another.

head slightly to the right, breathed out a swath of fire to encompass a section of the outlying district of Cerro Bonito, among whose rolling hills the estates of wealthy foreigners were situated. Dollops of flame dropping from the dragon's lip and from the jet of its exhalation ignited conflagrations in other sections of the city. The smell of the burning held an acrid chemical undertone that stung George's nostrils.

An animal fear possessed him, but the mental contract he had made to protect Peony enabled him to ignore both fear and pain. It may have been a blessing that he could not hear, for by the time he came to the foot of the hill, the greater portion of the city was on fire (only those areas adjoining and beneath the dragon were left untouched) and streams of panic-stricken people rushed past in the opposite direction, some bleeding and burned, their mouths open in what he assumed to be screams, a sound that would have encouraged his own nascent panic. The streams increased to a flood when he reached the outskirts of Morningshade. He had to fight his way through streets thronged by crowds surging toward the plain. Directly ahead, seen through the dust and across rooftops striped with rust, Griaule's foreleg sprouted from the slum like a thewy green-and-gold tree thrust up from an orchard in hell; his dirty white belly sagged low above the finial atop a four-story temple devoted to his worship, more like a billow in a giant's dirty bed sheet than a piece of sky. An alley opened between storefronts on George's left. He wedged through the crowd and stepped into it in order to formulate a plan of action without being jostled; however, once away from the turbulence of the crowd, the situation seemed hopeless and he understood he had taken on a fool's errand. He made ready to plunge back into the crowd, intending to join them in flight, but at the far end of the alley he spotted a sign bearing the crude painting of a cornucopia—the business that it advertised, a pawnshop, was close to Ali's. He could spare a moment, he told himself, before surrendering to fear. Peony loved Sylvia's fantasies about the brothel and, if she had survived, she might well have taken refuge in a place Sylvia described as home to a loving sisterhood. He raced along the alley, forged a path toward Ali's through the sparser crowds on the side street, and burst through the door.

A SCRAWNY, STOOP-SHOULDERED, white-haired man drinking two-handed at the bar was the sole occupant of the common room. Boards and benches had been overturned; bottles and broken crockery littered the floor. George's hearing had returned to a degree—his ears rang, but he could detect the brighter range of sounds. He asked if the old man had seen Peony and the man did not turn from the bar to confront George and gave no other response. Drying blood from one ear made a track down his seamed cheek. Then the walls shimmied, the floorboards bounced, dust sifted down from the rafters and more bottles fell from a shelf behind the counter—Griaule shifting position once again. Two steps and their world was in chaos.

Upstairs, George hurried along a corridor, throwing open the doors, giving the rooms a cursory inspection, finding unmade beds and nightgowns draped over chairs, but no Peony. He was certain that he would be crushed or incinerated, and that certainty grew stronger with each second. In a room at the end of the hall whose window framed a view of the city, ruddy light flickered on creamy wallpaper with a pyramid pattern, and a pudgy, dark-haired woman in a pink flannel robe sat on the edge of the bed, watching Teocinte burn. Her eyes fell upon him and an expression of mirth spread like butter melting across her features. She patted the sheet beside her, inviting him to sit. He wanted to urge her to run, but something in her face, some central weakness, told him not to bother. A muscular balding man pushed past him into the room and, after a hostile glance at George, removed his trousers. The woman turned again to the window, plucking fretfully at the lapel of her robe. Abandoning them to whatever exercise they planned, George fled down the stairs and out into the street, almost overlooking the slight ginger-haired figure squatting on her haunches outside the door, rocking back and forth. Peony didn't complain when he caught her up—she appeared stunned and uncaring.

Whereas the behavior of the couple in Ali's had impressed George as being utterly final in its dissolution, the streets were an evolution of that finality, a Babel of dimly perceived sounds and voices, a bedlam of people who clawed and clutched and kicked. At one point somebody knocked him off-balance, sending him to a knee; he put out a hand to prevent a fall and braced against the bruised, misshapen face of a boy who had been trampled beneath the feet of the crowd. He yanked back his hand, repelled, yet this intimate contact with death firmed his resolve and he became single-minded in his pursuit of survival, using his size to full advantage, treating people like impediments, clubbing them with his fist, shoving them down and tossing them aside without a thought for their fate or the state of his soul, stained by one death and now, doubtless, by others. Aghast faces surfaced from the melee and he dispatched them one after the other. Dust and the smell of fear, of fury...all the toxins of dementia poisoned the air. Yet he felt immune to fear, unstoppable, invincible in his lack of emotion. Then, as he reached the outskirts of the city, where the dirt street gave out onto an upward slope, the crowd fanning out across it, a splintering crack ripped across the other noises, seeming to come both from inside him and from without. George looked back and saw that the dragon's leg had buckled, a shockingly white shard of bone protruding from the scales above the knee, blood oozing from the break, and he recognized that Cattanay's prediction had come to pass.[13] Griaule's gargantuan head swiveled to the left, a malefic golden eye canted downward, and though others must have thought the same, George had the idea that the dragon was staring directly at him, a white star shining deep within his throat. The leg buckled further, the dragon listed toward them, and George sprinted up the hill, running even more desperately than before, carrying Peony under an arm like a small rolled-up rug. The crowd's wailing became a shriek as they fled from beneath Griaule's fall.

Perhaps time slowed, subject to a new gravity now that Griaule was truly dying, or perhaps it was simply the chemistry of terror stretching seconds into wider fractions; but George ran for what felt like a long, long time. He heard an eerie hiss and a blast of heat at his back sent him veering out of control; he righted himself and kept going. Time slowed further and he could clearly make out his labored breathing above the ringing in his ears and the shouts of people around him; and then, the last thing he would ever hear: the dragon's final roar, a percussive sound that shot lightning through his ears and resolved into a fizzing that banished every other sound, grew faint and fainter yet, then faded and faded,

---

13   Though he did not predict that Griaule would awaken, Cattanay told the city fathers that the poisons in the paint would seep into his system, weakening his internal structure, and, unable to support his weight, the dragon would eventually "cave in like an old barn."

stranding him in the midst of a pure unmodulated silence. The earth convulsed, twitching like the skin on a cat's back, and he was flung through the air, somehow managing to hang onto Peony and shield her from harm. He did not black out, but lay facedown for ten or fifteen minutes, longer perhaps, moving an arm, a leg, not testing his mobility, just incidental movements, content to rest and be thoughtless. When he sat up he found that Peony was unconscious, but breathing steadily. Only then did he turn and gaze through the pall of dust and smoke toward Teocinte.

The better sections of town, Cerro Bonito, Haver's Roost, and Yulin's Grove, were still afire, releasing black smoke into the sky from half a thousand conflagrations; but the shanties of Morningshade had gone up as if made of paper and all that was left of them were smoldering piles of wreckage; indeed, the blaze had moved through the slum at such a pace that a handful of more substantial buildings in the district, those with their own water supply (Griaule's temple for instance), had survived relatively unscathed, the fire sweeping past them so rapidly that they had not been endangered for long—presumably their staffs and inhabitants had taken steps to protect them. Dwarfing the ruinous landscape, the immensity that was Griaule lay on his side, his back toward the hill where George and Peony were situated, his neck twisted so that his snout angled toward the sky like a scaly tower, a forked tongue lolling between his fangs.

His ribcage had shattered and bones poked through the skin in five or six places. It was a sight of such scope and implausibility, George could not frame the whole picture in his mind and for years thereafter, until his actual memories were replaced by a popular rendering of the death of Griaule, he recalled it in fragments. The most memorable element of the scene for him was not Griaule, but the slope that led up from the outskirts of the city. Although the majority of the dead had been incinerated by the dragon's uncanny fire, reduced to piles of unidentifiable ash, his flame must have weakened toward the end, because several thousand carbonized corpses decorated the hill, replicas of their living selves save for the fact they were blackened and so fragile that the pressure of a finger upon them would cause them to collapse and loose their shape. They were dust held together by habit and little else, yet they looked solid, an intricate weaving together of human forms that might have been mistaken for a work accomplished by some apocalyptic artist.

Peony stirred; her fist opened—the scale slipped from her palm. George picked it up and was startled to feel that cold, crawly vitality he had become aware of in the thickets on the day he and Peony met. An image slipped into his mind, that of a gold coin, a Byzantine solidus, very rare, from the reign of the emperor Aleksii. Then an unfamiliar silver coin, yet Egyptian in aspect, came into his mind, and it was followed by another and another yet, and he saw gems of superb luster and clarity, golden cups of great antiquity beset with uncut stones, bejeweled daggers and mirrors with gold frames, a small mountain of such objects, a treasure like no other. He knew he should be about the business of survival (they were not safe yet), but he was tired and the gold was so alluring and that other world of death and smoke and flame seemed far away. And then he was exiting the cavern where the gold was kept, going by torchlight along a meandering tunnel, walking slowly and silently as in a dream, and once out in the light of day he could no longer see the entrance to the tunnel. It had vanished, hidden by ferns and vines and perhaps by some ancient magic, but he didn't concern himself with such trivia— he had the confidence, a serene sense of fate and his relation to it, that he would find his treasure again.

CHAPTER EIGHT

EXCERPT FROM THE
LAST DAYS OF GRIAULE
by Sylvia Monteverdi

HEY WERE AT HIM the next day, all the hustlers, the thieves, and the entrepreneurs, inclusive of those who had legal rights to his body and those who did not. Their awe annihilated by greed, a force nearly equal to fear, they swarmed over the corpse, cutting, prying, digging up the hillside where the dragon had rested, searching for his horde. In light of what had transpired, it was disgusting, but it was fascinating as well. I spent much of the next decade documenting the period in my books and stories about the town's rebirth and its newest industry, the sale and distribution of Griaule's relics, fraudulent and real. During that time I rarely left Teocinte, but almost eight years to the day after I had last seen George and Peony in the amphitheater, I was in Port Chantay on some protracted business with my publisher and, on a whim, I contacted George, inviting him and Peony for a glass of wine. He suggested we meet at Silk, a trendy waterfront café with wide glass windows, dainty tables and chairs, and no silk whatsoever apart from the woman whose name it bore.

I'd heard that they had both been deafened, that Peony suffered from amnesia and now lived with George as his ward, and that George, who had divorced, was quite wealthy—rumor had it that he had been the one to unearth Griaule's horde. It was also rumored that he had an improper relationship with Peony, though on the face of things they appeared to be a typical father-and-daughter. He slurred his words a bit due to his deafness, but otherwise appeared fit; he sported a mustache and a goatee (his hair had gone gray) that, along with a tailored suit and the fastidiousness that attended his movements, lent him a cultivated air. Yet his physical changes were nothing compared to the mental. Gone was every trace of the city bumpkin I had known, the insecurity, earnestness, the paranoia. He possessed a coolness of manner that was informed, I thought, by an utter absence of emotionality, and this unnerved me. I would not have trusted myself to be able to control him as once I had.

Drastic as these changes were, Peony's were even more extreme. She had developed into beautiful, poised young woman who was, in every respect, quite charming. George claimed that her amnesia had wiped out all memory of abuse and thus had assisted in her maturation. Her attempts at speech were difficult to understand, for she did not recall the sound of words, and she relied on sign language to communicate, with George serving as her interpreter. After an exchange of pleasantries, she apologized for having forgotten me and went to have coffee with a friend at an outside table, leaving George and I to talk.

"Monteverdi," he said. "I don't suppose that is your real name."

"Of course not! What would I be without an alias?"

I had meant this as a joke, but George did not smile—he nodded as if my statement had revealed some essential truth about me, and this caused me think that perhaps it had.

"I'm sorry I didn't try to find you," I said. "After the fire and everything."

"It was chaos," said George. "You would have been wasting your time."

"That wasn't why I didn't look for you."

"Oh?"

"I was afraid you were falling in love with me."

He nodded thoughtfully. "I could have fallen in love with almost anyone in those days. You happened to be in the right place at the right time."

"And you were acting crazy. At least you were before Griaule herded us back to Teocinte. I didn't want to be around you."

George let four or five seconds elapse before smiling thinly and saying, "Well, you're safe from me now."

"I don't feel safe." I waited for a response, but none came. "You make me uneasy."

"Peony says I often have that effect on other people. In your case, I imagine it's exacerbated by guilt."

"Guilt? What would I have to be guilty about? I did nothing..."

"It's not important," he said. "Really. It's quite trivial."

"I want to know what you're accusing me of!"

"Not at thing. Forget I mentioned it." He reached a hand into a side pocket of his jacket as if to withdraw something, but let it hang there. "I've read the little book you wrote about us."

I was irritated, yet at the same time curious to know what he thought about my work. "And how did it strike you?"

"Accurate," he said. "As far as it went. I was as you initially described me. Desperate. Desperate to escape my old life. But I would never have admitted it then."

"What do you mean, '...as far as it went?'"

"You missed the best part of the story."

"I saw enough of Griaule's death, if that's what you're talking about. What's more, I've seen the city rebuilt, which you didn't see."

"The city's of no consequence. As for Griaule..." He chuckled. "We've always underestimated him. By hacking him apart and carrying the pieces to the far corners of the earth, we did exactly what he wanted. Now he rules in every quarter of the globe."

"I beg your pardon?"

"You once quoted me a passage from Rossacher. Do you remember? 'His thoughts roam the plenum, his mind is a cloud that encompasses our world.' Something of an overstatement, yet it's true enough. Do you find it so hard to accept now?"

"Are you telling me Griaule is alive? Bodiless...or alive in all his separate parts?"

He inclined his head and made a delicate gesture with his hand, as if to suggest that he had no interest in pursuing the matter.

I drained the dregs of my wine. "Don't you find it strange that we've reversed roles? I was once the believer and you the skeptic."

He took his hand from his pocket and held it out, his palm open to display a glass pendant in which was embedded a chip of lustrous blue-green, darkening to a dull azurine blue at the edges.

"Is that my scale?" I asked.

"Peony and I have no further use for it. I think Griaule intended it to be yours."

The glass enclosing the scale was cold and somewhat tingly to the touch. I remarked on this and George said, "It may be that I am mad, and that Peony is mad, and that we have not been guided in our lives ever since Griaule was disembodied. You can prove this one way or the other by shattering he glass and touching the scale. The sensation will be much stronger that way."

"Will it reveal the location of the Griaule's horde?" I asked half in jest.

"Too late for that," he said. "But he will have something for you, I'm sure. Since we met, everything in our lives has been part of Griaule's design."

I tucked the scale into my purse. "Perhaps you can explain, since you seem so certain in your knowledge, why he deemed it necessary to uproot so many people and drive us onto the plain. Was it simply to witness his death, or was it something more?"

"I have come to understand Griaule to an extent, but I can't know everything he knows. Was it ego, the desire to have at least a few survivors who could bear witness to his death? Yes, I think so. But there is much more to it than that. If he wishes he can control every facet of our lives. And our lives—yours and mine and Peony's, and thousands of others besides—have been thus controlled. We are part of a scheme by means of which he will someday come to dominate the world as Rossacher's book claimed he already had. So far, the instrumentality he's used to implement his scheme has been unwieldy, scattershot. He's made mistakes. Now that he is everywhere in the world, his manipulations will grow more subtle, more precise, and he will make no further mistakes. Eventually, I assume we will be unaware of him ...and he will lose interest in us. It may be that this is, by necessity, how the relationships between men and gods develop." George fussed with his napkin and said in a reproachful tone, as if talking to a child, "You knew all this once. Have you truly forgotten?"

"Forgotten? Perhaps I place less value on the specific precepts of my belief than once I did, but no, I haven't forgotten."

George was silent for a while, silent and motionless, and I thought how restrained he had grown in his movements; yet he did not seem constrained or repressed in the least—rather it was as though he had become accustomed to stillness. He cleared his throat, took a sip of wine, and said, "Let us speak no more of it." He nudged the menu with a finger, turning it so he could more read the front page. "Shall I order something? The seaweed cakes are excellent here...and the cherries confit would go well with your port."

✠

WHEN IT CAME time for George to leave, I felt strong emotion—we had been through an ordeal together and our conversation had, despite his coolness, brought back fond memories I did not think I had—I would have liked to acknowledge the experience with an embrace and I expected George to feel the same way, but he performed a slight bow, collected Peony, and left without a backward glance.

I have not yet broken the glass in which the scale is encased, yet I know someday I will, if only to satisfy my curiosity about George. I ran into him and Peony once more before returning to Teocinte. Two days following our meeting at Silk, I took the morning air on the promenade, looking at the boats in the harbor, their exotic keels and bright, strangely shaped sails giving evidence of Port Chantay's international flavor, and caught sight of George and Peony by the railing that fronted the water, engaged in what appeared to be a spirited conversation...at least it was spirited on Peony's part. I ducked behind a small palm tree, one of many potted specimens set along the promenade, not wishing to be seen. We'd said our farewells, as belated and anti-climactic as they were, and I felt rejected—I'd come to the meeting prepared to rebuff George's advances and had not expected to be treated with diffidence. If his cool manner had been studied, I would have chalked all he said and did up to hurt feelings; but his dismissive behavior had seemed wholly unaffected.

His back to the water, George leaned against the railing, his hands braced and his face tipped to the sun like a penitent at prayer, while Peony moved about him with quick steps, almost a dance, pacing to and fro, making graceful turns and exuberant gestures. I imagined her to be describing an event that had thrilled or elated her; but as I watched, though there was no overt change in their physical attitudes, I started to view them differently and perceived sexual elements in the dance—it reminded me of Griaule's temple in Morningshade and how some of my sisters in the brothel would circle the dragon's statue, caressing it from time to time. There is a sexual component in every young girl's connection with her father and I'm sure that was all it was between George and Peony...even if not, she was twenty-one, old enough to do as she pleased. Like most people, I needed to think meanly about something I valued in order to walk away from it, especially something I had neglected for no good reason and such a stretch of years; so I chose to think about George and Peony as having an illicit relationship and told myself it was none of my business what they did or which god they worshiped or how they went through the world, because they were unimportant to me. Perhaps those feelings and memories that surfaced during our meeting were, as are many of our recollections, born of a marriage between false emotion and a lack of clarity concerning the facts. Perhaps our lives are contrivances of lies and illusions. Yet when I think now about George and Peony, none of this seems relevant and scarcely the day passes when I do not call them to mind.